# A TRIP THROUGH

# Airport

## Table of Contents

Rigby

# A Busy Place...

Tickets, suitcases, security checks, and people. Walkways, runways, jetways, and people. From London to New York, or from Tokyo to Melbourne, people around the world rely on airplanes to travel.

An airport is a very busy place. There are so many people, with so many places to go. How does everybody get where they want to go? Let's explore an airport and find out. Do you have your suitcase packed? **Let's go!**

# How an Airport Works

## ① Moving
*the People*

## ② Loading
*the Baggage*

# ③ Preparing *the Airplane*

# ④ Moving *the Airplane*

# ① Moving
## *the People*

Boarding pass with gate number

When we arrive at the **terminal**, our first stop is the ticket counter. We check in our suitcases. We get a boarding pass with our gate number on it. Now we have to find our gate! That's where the plane is waiting.

**Is my plane on time?**

Signs show us which way to go. TV screens tell us if the plane is on time. Our gate is far away! We can get there quickly and safely on a moving sidewalk called a **walkway**.

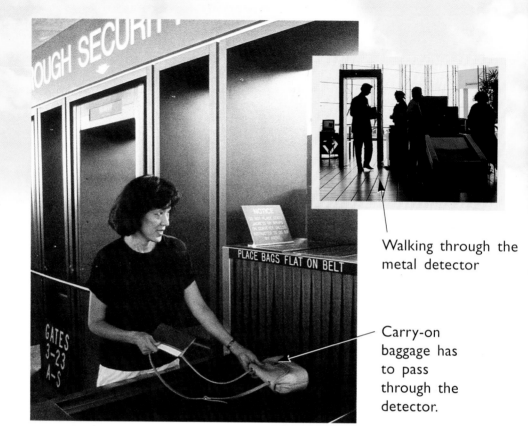

Walking through the metal detector

Carry-on baggage has to pass through the detector.

Empty your pockets! All passengers go through the metal detector before they get to the gates. If the metal detector finds dangerous objects, it will signal airport **security**.

Carry-on bags are placed on a **conveyor belt** and moved through an X-ray machine. The X-ray machine allows security to see what's inside the bags.

There's the gate! We have to show our boarding pass to go onto the **jetway.** The airplane is at the end of the jetway. Welcome aboard! I get the seat by the window!

The jetway fits snugly against the plane.

# ② Loading
## *the Baggage*

Back at the ticket counter, our suitcases get their own special tickets. We keep one part of the ticket until we meet our suitcases again at the end of the trip. The part that is attached to the suitcase has a special three-letter code. The code stands for the airport where the suitcase will go. I hope we both make it to the same place!

The suitcases are put on a conveyor belt, which takes them to a sorting area. Laser cameras read the ticket codes to sort the baggage. Big paddles push the suitcases toward **cargo** boxes that are carried on small trucks.

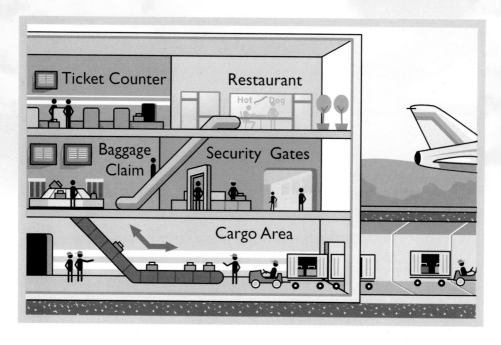

The trucks carry the cargo boxes to the airplane through an underground tunnel. That way, the trucks won't get in our way as we go to the plane. When the truck gets to the plane, the cargo boxes are unloaded.

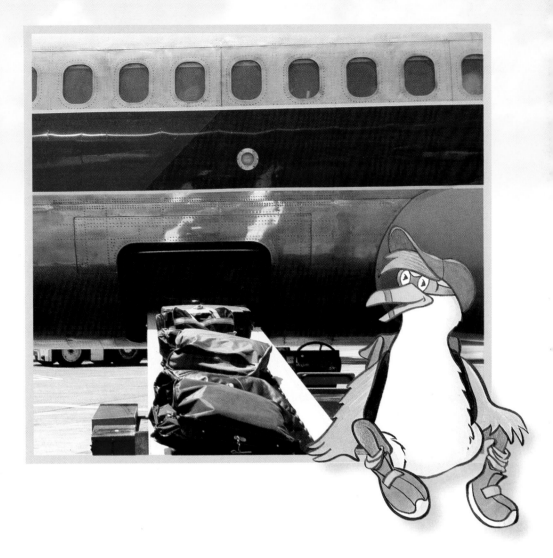

The suitcases move up another conveyor belt and into the cargo hold of the plane. The cargo hold is underneath the part of the plane where we sit. Now our suitcases are ready to go. Do they get a window seat, too?

# ③ Preparing
## *the Airplane*

Checking the engines

Fuel the plane. Load the food and water. Check the engines. Check the flight panel. These jobs take place after a plane lands and before it takes off again. This in-between time is called **turnaround.**

FUEL ✓
FOOD.
WATER ✓

ENGINES

Turnaround is carefully planned work that prepares a plane for its next flight. Workers must do their jobs quickly and carefully to safely prepare the airplane.

Our airplane needs fuel. The driver of a **pumper truck** attaches a hose to the plane's fuel tank. The other end of the hose hooks into an underground fuel tank. Fill 'er up!

Smaller airports may not have underground fuel tanks. Above-ground tanks and fuel tanker trucks are used to fill the airplanes at these airports.

Trucks use lifts to move the food trays into the kitchen of the airplane. Large hoses carry drinking water from another truck to the airplane's water tank.

We forgot to pack our lunch! Lucky for us, the flight attendants serve snacks, sandwiches, and juice.

The most important part of turnaround is making sure the plane is safe for another flight. Workers test the airplane's mechanical parts and computer systems. The pilot checks the radios and controls in the **cockpit**. All systems are go!

# ④ Moving
## *the Airplane*

A small truck called a **tug** pushes the airplane back from the jetway. Then our pilot calls ground control on the radio. Ground control tells the pilot which **runway** to use. The pilot taxis the airplane to the right runway.

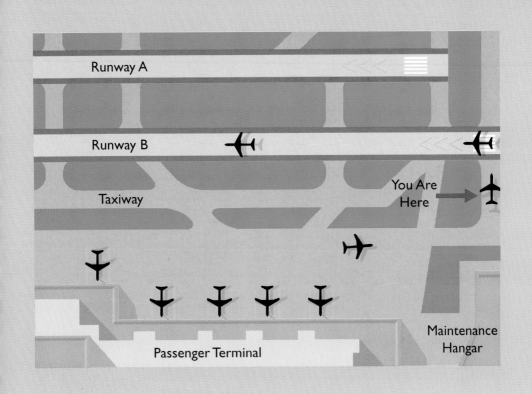

Runway A

Runway B

Taxiway

You Are Here

Maintenance Hangar

Passenger Terminal

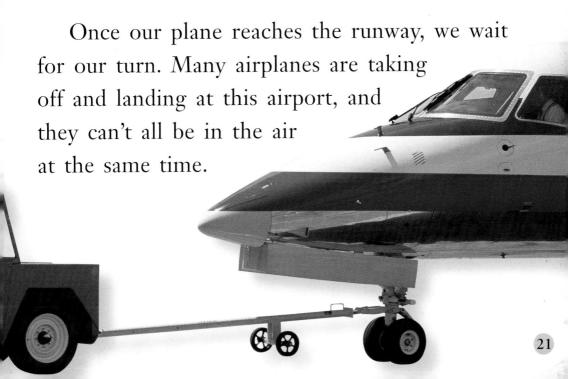

Once our plane reaches the runway, we wait for our turn. Many airplanes are taking off and landing at this airport, and they can't all be in the air at the same time.

Air traffic controllers inside the control tower direct all the airplanes. They keep the planes moving on time and in order. Each person in the tower has a special job to do. Some talk to the pilots over radios. Others use radar and computers to track the airplanes in the sky.

# Take-Off!

The passengers are in their seats. The baggage is loaded. The plane

is prepared. The pilot is ready. The control tower says, "Flight 959, you're cleared for take-off."

*Good-bye!*

Shalom!

**Ciao!**

**Adios!**

Bon Voyage!

# Glossary

**cargo**  the bags and boxes carried by an airplane

**cockpit**  the front part of the airplane where the controls are and where the pilot sits

**conveyor belt**  a moving band that carries things from one place to another

**jetway**  a tunnel that connects an airplane to the airport terminal

**pumper truck**  a cart that connects the airplane to the fuel tanks

**runway**  the cement road used for take-off and landing at an airport

**security**  airport police

**terminal**  the airport building

**tug**  a truck that pulls the airplane out to the runway

**turnaround**  the time between when a plane lands and when it takes off again

**walkway**  a moving sidewalk